Great Big Guinea Pigs

Susan L. Roth

BLOOMSBURY
CHILDREN'S
BOOKS

For Jesse with love

Typeset in Paradigm Bold. Art created with collage.

Design by Nicole Gastonguay

Published
by Bloomsbury
Publishing,
New York,
London, and Berlin
Distributed to the trade by
Holtzbrinck Publishers

Library of Congress
Cataloging-in-Publication Data
Roth, Susan L.
Great big guinea pigs /
by Susan Roth.— 1st U.S. ed.
p. cm.
Summary: A guinea pig tells her child the true story of giant guinea pigs that lived in Venezuela about eight million years ago.
ISBN-10: 1-58234-724-7
ISBN-13: 978-1-58234-724-0
[1. Guinea pigs—Fiction. 2. Prehistoric animals—Fiction.]
I. Title.
PZ10.3.R747Gre 2006
[E]—dc22
2006000970

First U.S. Edition 2006
Printed in China
1 3 5 7 9 10 8 6 4 2

Bloomsbury Publishing,
Children's Books, U.S.A.
175 Fifth Avenue, New York, NY 10010

All papers used by Bloomsbury Publishing are natural, recyclable products made from wood grown in well-managed forests. The manufacturing processes conform to the environmental regulations of the country of origin.

"Tell me a story. One more
story before I go to sleep."

"What kind of story?"

"NOT a made-up story."

"A TRUE story?"

"Yes."

"All right, just one more."

"Once upon a time, about eight million years ago, guinea pigs like us weren't sweet, cute, and little. We didn't live in cages and people didn't take care of us. No one put pine chips and clean newspaper on the floor every day. No one brought us fresh water or seeds and berries from the pet store. No one gave us chewing

sticks, and there were no such things as exercise wheels. No one brought us to school for show and tell, and no children yelled, 'Can I hold him? Can I hold him? Come on, let ME! It's my turn.' In those days, NO ONE would have wanted to hold us."

"Why not?"

"Because we were wild animals! We took care of ourselves, outdoors, just like all the other wild animals. We were GREAT BIG GUINEA PIGS!"

"Were we as big as dogs?"

"Dogs? We were bigger than houses!"

"Oh, Mom, we were NOT."

"Well, maybe not houses. But we were bigger than goats. We were bigger than horses! We were as big as buffalo! We were giants."

"How much did we weigh?"

"Almost a ton."

"What did we eat?"

"Back then, we ate nothing but grass."

"Yuck! How could we get so big eating grass?"

"Please don't talk with your mouth full."

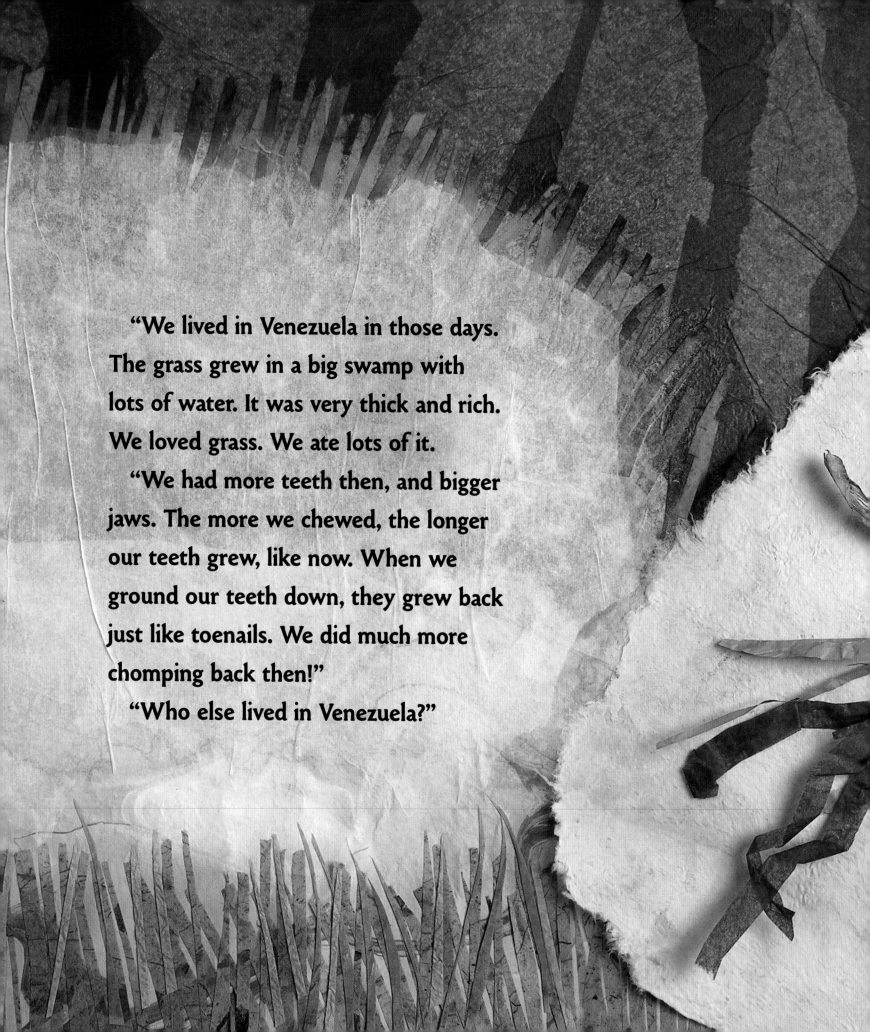

"We lived in Venezuela in those days. The grass grew in a big swamp with lots of water. It was very thick and rich. We loved grass. We ate lots of it.

"We had more teeth then, and bigger jaws. The more we chewed, the longer our teeth grew, like now. When we ground our teeth down, they grew back just like toenails. We did much more chomping back then!"

"Who else lived in Venezuela?"

"Lots of animals. Great big ones, like us. In those days, there were giant catfish, huge turtles, tall birds, and long alligators. It was crowded because everyone was so big. We had to watch out, too, because sometimes those very long alligators got hungry for guinea pigs."

"OH!"

"But mostly everyone had plenty to eat, and we were happy in our big grassy swamp."

"What did we do besides eat?"

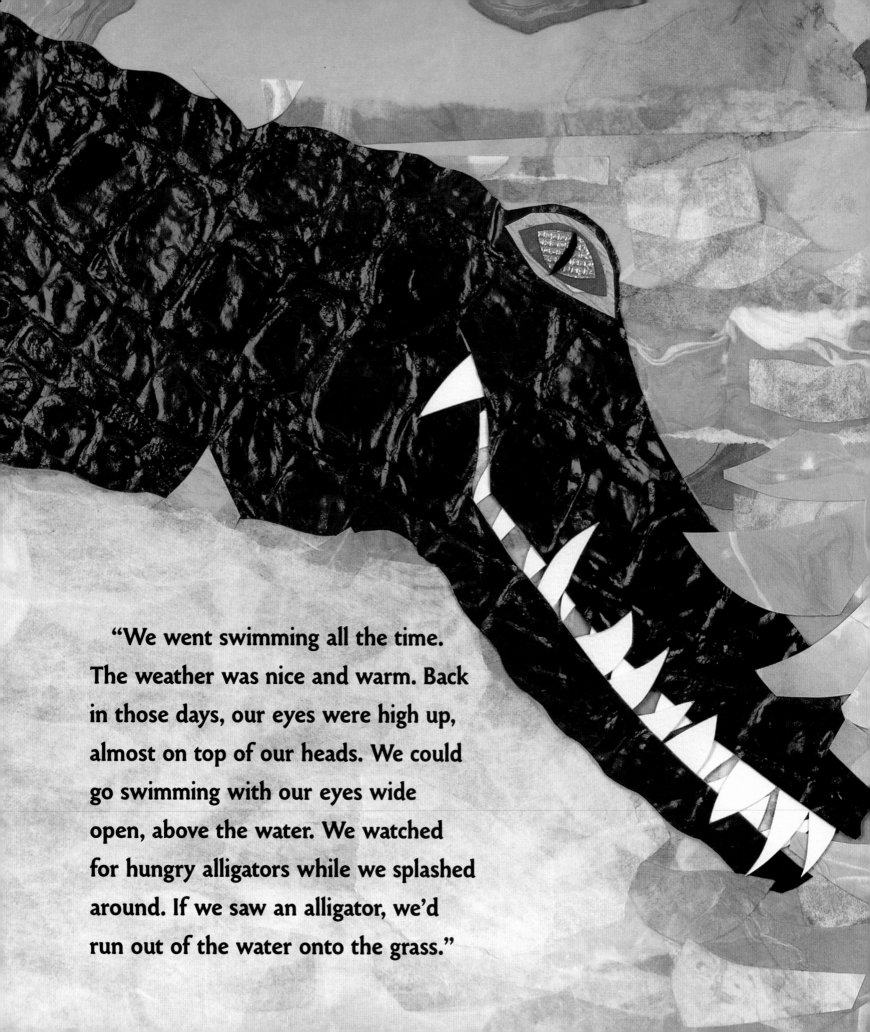

"We went swimming all the time. The weather was nice and warm. Back in those days, our eyes were high up, almost on top of our heads. We could go swimming with our eyes wide open, above the water. We watched for hungry alligators while we splashed around. If we saw an alligator, we'd run out of the water onto the grass."

"We usually walked upright back then. We had very strong back legs, and longer tails, too. Our tails helped us to balance, the way tails help kangaroos nowadays."

In those days, we were too big and too heavy to jump. I think one reason we changed so much over the years was that we couldn't run fast enough."

"Why did we have to run?"

"Well, things were fine for about five million years. But then the bottom of the ocean started to poke through the water, and a landbridge formed. Soon, North American animals were traveling south."

"Then what happened?"

"No one knows for sure, but our food probably began to disappear since the new animals had started eating it, too. Over the years, we ate less. We got smaller and quicker. We needed to run fast to get away from the fiercer, hungrier animals."

"And then what happened?"

"Some of us stayed wild. We still have some wild relatives. But many, like you and me, got cuter and friendlier, so children wanted to keep us as pets."

"Don't you wish we still lived in the swamp in Venezuela? We could go swimming every day."

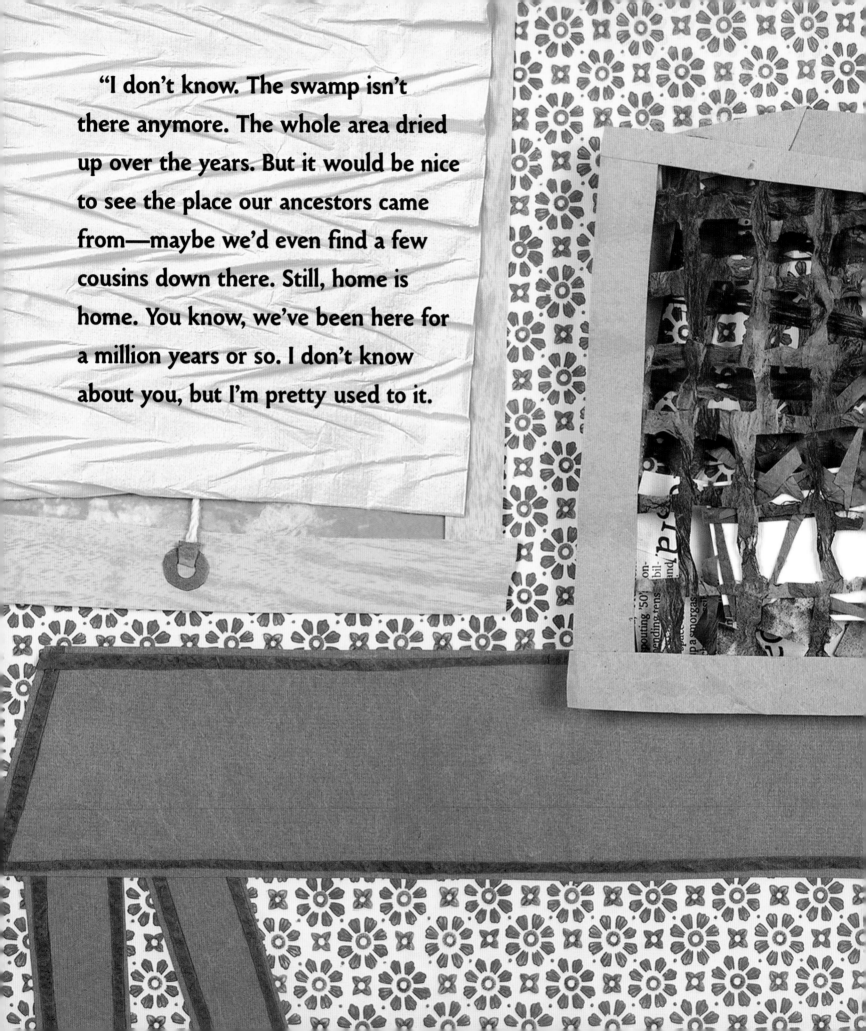

"I don't know. The swamp isn't there anymore. The whole area dried up over the years. But it would be nice to see the place our ancestors came from—maybe we'd even find a few cousins down there. Still, home is home. You know, we've been here for a million years or so. I don't know about you, but I'm pretty used to it.

"And now it's time for all guinea pigs, great big wild ones and sweet little baby ones, to close their eyes and go to sleep."

"I don't think that was a TRUE story!"

"It certainly was."

"How do you know it was true?"

"I read about it this morning in the *Times*. Tomorrow morning, I'll read it to you. You'll have to wake up early, though, before the people clean our cage and change the newspaper."

Bibliography

Alexander, R. McNeill. "A Rodent as Big as a Buffalo." *Science* Vol. 301 No. 5640 (19 Sept. 2003): 1678–1679.

Bawoll, Karen. *A New Owner's Guide to Guinea Pigs*. Neptune, NJ: T.F.H. Publications, 2001.

Gorman, James. "Distinctly Big, if Extinct: The 1,500-Pound Rodent." *The New York Times* 19 Sept. 2003: 8.

Sánchez-Villagra, Marcelo R., Orangel Aguilera, and Inés Horovitz. "The Anatomy of the World's Largest Extinct Rodent." *Science* Vol. 301 No. 5640 (19 Sept. 2003): 1708–1710.

Vergano, Dan. "Gigantic Prehistoric 'Guinea Pig' Fossils Discovered." *USA Today* 18 Sept. 2003: A1.

Author's note

Thank you to my mother, who heard the text first and laughed. Thank you also to Annie Athanassakis, Sharon Cresswell, the Epstein family, Olga R. Guartan, Hans-Ulrich Haering, Nobuko and Masato Kasuga, Karen Leggett, Nancy Patz, Mary Quattlebaum, Marcelo Sánchez-Villagra, Jill Tarlau, and George Michael Weiss. Thank you J.R., A.A.A.H., E.T.L., and P. And thank you to my friends at Bloomsbury for their enthusiasm as well as for their patience.

Facts about guinea pigs

Some guinea pig–lovers suggest that newspapers make the best cage liners. Others think that newsprint can be toxic for guinea pigs; they use pine or cedar chips.

The majority of guinea pigs are domesticated, and all the great big guinea pigs are extinct. Other large rodents do exist, including the capybara, now the world's largest rodent, found in Central and South America.